CHICKYPOOH ™

"Hi, I'm Chickypooh. I'm the chick with a leash on my kitty. Follow me, read my book series as I tour city to city."

"I want to teach you ways to protect yourself and to abstain. Abstain means to resist anything improper. Don't do it. Refrain!"

"There's an abundance of wisdom, knowledge, illustrations, rhymes, and reasons to turn this page. No matter your race, creed, or if your 9 to 99 in age."

"My advice is obvious; you'll see. By applying it, it will help to set you free."

ACKNOWLEDGEMENTS

We gratefully acknowledge all organizations who are working diligently to protect women and children and to provide treatment to those who domestic violence has tremendously affected their lives.

CHICKYPOOH ™

THE BULLY WHO SLEEPS WITH MY MOMMY!

What Should We Do?

Jacqueline Charmane

GENRE: REALISTIC FICTION

This book is a work of realistic fiction. All information and opinions expressed herein are the views of the author. This publication is not intended to provide accurate and authoritative information concerning the subject matter covered and is for informational purposes only. Neither the author nor the publisher is attempting to provide legal advice of any kind.

THE BULLY WHO SLEEPS WITH MY MOMMY ~ What Should We do?
Copyright@2020 by Jacqueline Charmane
All Rights Reserved
PRINT ISBN: 978-0-9974496-8-6

Publication: February 2020

Published by The JC Collection

DEDICATION

This book is dedicated to those who have experienced domestic violence; either as a bully or victim. Bullying behavior is unacceptable. By exposing the behavior, we are sending a world-wide message that says, "we see you, we know you, and we want to help you."

The first time that it happened, I will never, ever forget.

I was playing with my Easy Bake Oven when I heard him holla, "You bit...."!

I didn't know the meaning of the word or the purpose of the rage.

I responded, though, like most kids would respond who are at my age.

I forgot all about what was in the oven and ran to find out what was wrong.

Unfortunately, to see the nature of the problem didn't take me very long.

Before I could get to the commotion,
I heard another piercing scream.

It was my mommy pleading, "Please,
don't hit me again! It's not what it
seems."

I cried out loud, "Mommy, what's
wrong?" But, to my dismay.

There my mommy was on the bathroom
floor crying profusely where she lay.

Weak from the fight, she whispered for me to go straight to my room.

I was so scared that I ran faster than a witch at night flying on her broom.

I curled up on my bed and closed my bedroom door tight.

I prayed that he would stop hurting my mommy with all of my might.

I heard one scream after another, followed by my mommy's plea.

"No, please stop. You're badly hurting me. Can't you see?"

All kinds of terrible thoughts ran through my scared-naïve mind.

What if he killed my mommy or caused her to go blind?

Who would love me and take care of me until I could?

Who would read to me and dress me as a mother should?

I was only nine years old; therefore, it would be a difficult task for me.

I even get incredibly sick when stunk by a pesky bumblebee.

I don't know how to correctly tie my shoes so that I don't trip or fall.

Who would play hide and seek with me, or help me hit a softball?

Riding a bike without training wheels
for me is very hard.

I always end up running over flowers
in the neighbor's yard.

Who would bandage and kiss my
skinned knee, elbow, and leg?

Who would make my grits with cheese,
sausage, and a fried egg?

I kept wishing that someone would come to take my mommy and me far, far away.

Maybe we could hide in a tree house from this man that hits her almost every day.

We'll have a spot light on to alert us if he comes near.

The spot light will also serve to let us know when the coast is clear.

We'll also make a sign that says, "Keep Away From Mommy And Me!"

We'll move the ladder so that he won't be able to climb the tree.

We'll be safe from this monster that she thought at first was kind.

Going forward I hope my mommy will look for a man that will love her as she was designed.

I remember how this horrible lifestyle for my mommy first got started.

It was when my daddy, whom I miss so much, one day departed.

After which it was difficult for my mommy to make ends meet.

There was no more candy, cookies, cakes, or my favorite treat.

For a while, it was my mommy and me living what she calls hand-to-mouth.

In hopes of finding a better life, she moved us to a state in the deep South.

I wanted daddy to come with us if only he could.

Mommy said he got locked up because of selling dope in the hood.

She took me once to see him in the state prison down the street.

I remember how the cells closing behind us made a catchy beat.

I overheard daddy saying to mommy, "I'm in here because of you!"

"If you hadn't been so greedy, I wouldn't have gone back doing jobs with the crew!"

Mommy yelled, "taking responsibility for your own choices is the mature thing to do."

"Until you face up to your wrongs, we are through."

"I don't ever again want to have anything to do with you and your dope."

"Take my advice, as I walk out of your life, don't drop the soap!"

That's the last time I saw my daddy as I remember his bright orange suit.

I thought to myself that's a color I don't ever want to wear in exchange for any amount of loot.

Mommy instantly ran to the store to play the number on daddy's back.

She's lost so much money from gambling, that it's hard to keep track.

My desire for daddy to come with us to the South was because I miss him so much.

He was the only dad on our block to jump with my girlfriends in double Dutch.

Can her dad come out to play?

All my friends would ask my mommy if my dad could come out to play.

I thought that was what they should ask her for me to play with them each day.

18

I liked it when my daddy would call me his favorite little squirt.

I didn't like it though when he would spank me because it hurt.

He would then walk away crying because he says that it hurt him more than it hurt me.

I couldn't understand how that could be when I was the one across his knee.

I never saw daddy hit mommy or heard him call her any awful names.

It was just that he couldn't seem to find and keep an honest job, so he claims.

Mommy always complained that there wasn't any food in the house to eat.

We always ran out of bread, eggs, milk, cheese, and every kind of meat.

Daddy would go out with no money
and, in hours, come home with bags
of food.

Mommy would make his favorite
meal, which she knew was a big bowl
of beef stewed.

Mommy never asked if the food was stolen or bought with illegal money.

She just turned on the charm, wrapped him in her arms then called him honey.

I didn't understand how one minute she'd argue with daddy about the company he kept.

All the time, she would sneak in his wallet to take his money as he slept.

Once daddy was gone,
it was evident that
mommy missed him too.

She would look at his
picture on the table and
cry boohoo.

The bills got further behind. Until one day, the sheriff banged on our front door.

I said, "Mommy, who's that?" She replied, "be quiet and get down on the floor!"

Unfortunately, we were three rent payments and two court dates too late to hide.

We heard a key turning in the door, so we snuck out the window on the side.

With two full black trash bags of clothes in each of her hands,

mommy and I headed to the deep South as those were her plans.

Once there, Mommy vowed we would never be homeless anymore.

She decided to do whatever it took to keep us from being poor.

HOMELESS PLEASE HELP!

She made tough choices for us to live every day.

She was determined to have food, clean clothes, and a decent place to stay.

She worked late each night without coming home to tuck me into bed.

That's because she wanted to make sure she kept a roof over my head.

Mommy told me never to tell anyone that she left me at nine years old by myself.

She would secure the door and put everything in my reach on a bottom shelf.

At first, I was scared to be home alone, but then I got very brave.

I knew how to make a sandwich and put leftovers in the microwave.

27

Mommy read to me a book about fire safety in the house.

As she read it, I was as quiet and attentive as a mouse.

It said in case of an emergency to call the police by dialing 911.

In case of a fire, I should crawl to safety then stand up and run.

Never play with matches, lighters, candles or an open flame.

Once they get out of control they can't be tamed.

Fire Safety In The House

The Lee Family

I still couldn't fall sound to sleep until mommy came through the door.

Some nights I would lay like a zombie on my bedroom floor.

When she would come in, I would quickly jump in the bed without a peep.

I could hear voices whispering, then mommy saying, "please be quiet, my daughter's asleep"!

It sounded like a man, so I peeked out to see if daddy had gotten out of jail.

It was a man but not my daddy, just some big, ugly, blue-hair male.

The way he touched my mommy he seemed disrespectful, to say the least.

He reminded me of a terrifying untamed historic ravenous beast.

He had hands like gigantic paws, little legs, and odd feet.

He was green with ripped clothing that wasn't very neat.

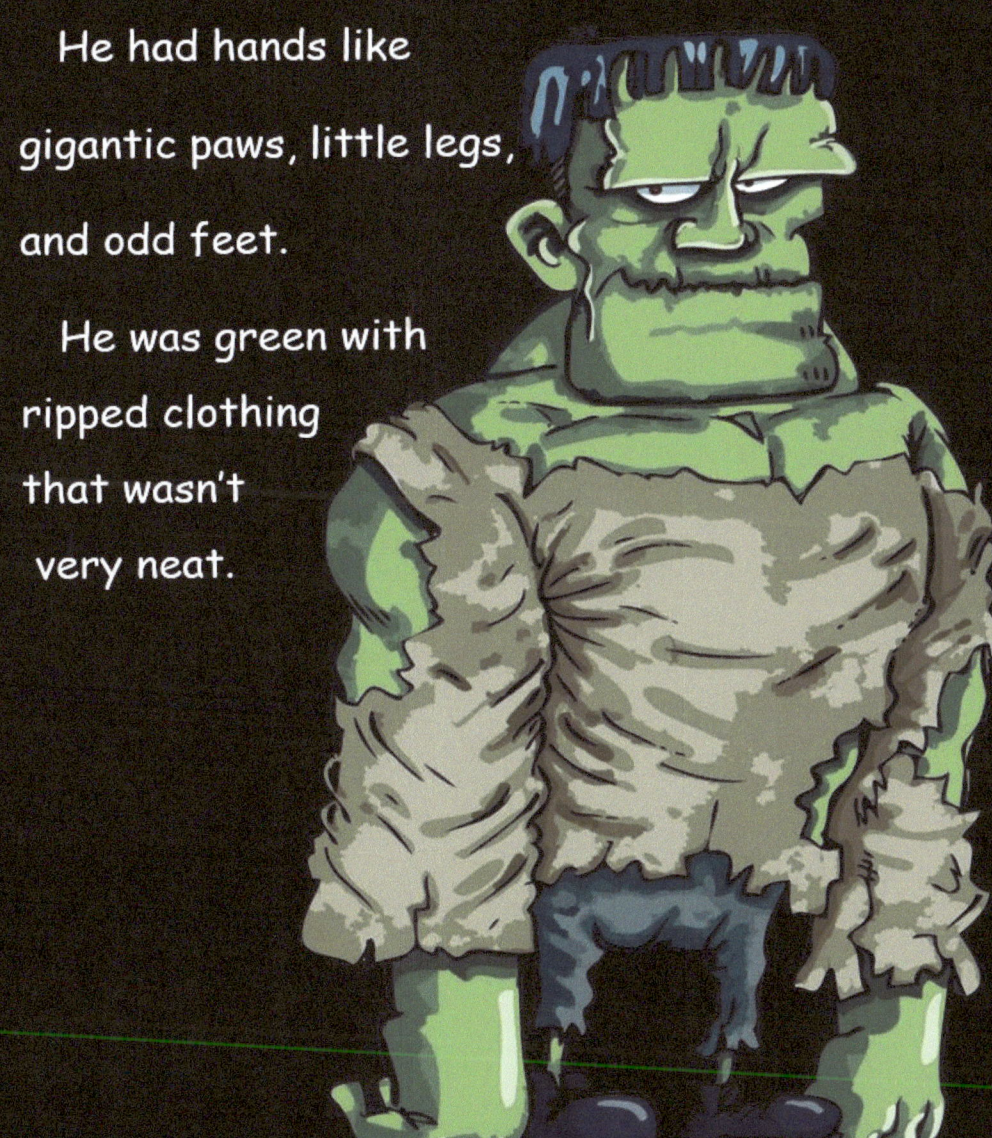

That's what that one looked like that came home with mommy this night.

All the other ones from weeks before were also a horrific sight.

There's been so many men and women that I've lost count of them all.

I could hear the noise that they made through my bedroom wall.

It made me so sad to think about it that I would cry myself to sleep.

I would pray to God to please protect my mommy and her soul to keep.

There was one man who came with mommy more often than the others.

He looked so much like my daddy; you would think that they were brothers.

If he is my daddy's brother, that will make him my uncle just as mommy said.

But is it right for uncles to later sleep with the woman that their brothers wed?

He was tall, with the kind of beard that any woman would love.

He appeared to be kind and, most importantly, gentler than a dove.

He started coming during the day, not just with mommy late at night

He even took the time to tuck me in, and as I slept, he'd turn out the light.

For the first time in a long time, mommy could get her hair styled and buy things that we needed.

She was happy that we moved to the South because her expectation was exceeded.

There is one thing my grand mom use to say about happiness obtained through material things.

It can quickly disappear like the dew in the morning that a light misty rain brings.

The dew looks so pretty as it rests gently upon each blade of a green mowed lawn.

But, when the scorching sun arises, in seconds, the luster to the grass is gone.

Unfortunately, each day I could see my so-called uncle showing signs of an abusive man.

One time he yelled at my mommy, then blacken her eye with a cast-iron frying pan.

That brings us to the beginning of this not unusual domestic violence tale.

Unfortunately, it happens to women of all walks of life—not just those who are meek, defenseless, or frail.

So that you understand the warning signs to look for in potential abusers,

I'll let my friend, Chickypooh, tell you how to recognize who she calls losers.

Hi, I'm Chickypooh, the bold chick with a leash on her kitty.

Men who are abusers, like flies, can be found in every city.

I say they're losers because women possess the courage to win.

A woman wins over her abuser when she recognizes her priceless value therein.

Women weren't meant to be bullied, humiliated, and beaten upon by men.

One-minute things seem well between them; then another she's scared out of her skin.

It's essential to know and to hold tight to your self-esteem.

Remember your morals, principals, and continue to reach for your dream.

Here are a few critical signs of a potentially violent person.

Accept the facts then move on before things worsen.

Abusers often follow a pattern of behavior that are warning signs.

They play with your emotions with tears and words that are sucker lines.

Words like, I didn't mean it, and I won't do it again, are apart of the bullying role.

Forgive them, then make safety for you and your children your ultimate goal.

Abusers often rush through the get-to-know-you stage to avoid you knowing about their past.

They may disguise this so-called romantic behavior by saying, "I can't live without you" or, "I found the right one at last!"

It's best to know a person through the ups and downs of various seasons.

That will allow you to see how they emotional respond and their reasons.

The seasons I'm referring to aren't Winter, Spring, Summer, or Fall.

They're the changes in their life that makes them either humble or to brawl.

Fighting is a way for abusers to attempt to stay in control.

It's also their means of keeping you in a subservient role.

In addition, abusers get physical when they feel like their backs are against a wall.

They most likely may have a history of past violence and are violent overall.

Abusers are jealous of your relationships with others, such as co-workers, family, and friends.

They want your trust in only them so that they know where you are during the week and weekends.

Isolating you breaks down
and eventually eliminates your
support system.

If you attempt to leave
without help, the abusers goal
is for you to come back
because you miss him.

Always maintain a few platonic
relationships of those who love
and care for you.

They're the ones who,
through trials and tribulations,
will help see you through.

PICTURE PERFECT

FRIENDS FOREVER

Abusers attempt to control your transportation to say where you can and cannot go.

They'll give you money freely just to be in charge of your cash flow.

They then feel they have the right to ask you questions such as, "where've you been" and "what did you buy?"

These questions aren't to show interest but are used as a way for them to spy.

Last but not least, verbal abuse usually starts long before physical battering.

You can appear your very best, but from your abuser, you get no flattering.

Instead, you're too fat, too skinny, too ugly, and your hair is an absolute mess.

You'll find when you're around a mental abuser you're always under stress.

I could go on and on disclosing the signs of an abuser that you may experience each day.

However, it's your conscience that will expose you to the dangers where you stay.

Don't turn a death hear to what you hear your abuser say.

Stay focused on your health and well-being each and every day.

It's never too late to start your life over from a safe physical and mental place.

Time and love heals all wounds when you put yourself in a positive space.

Don't be concern about what may happen when you pack your bags and leave.

All things work together, the good with the bad, if with your heart you believe.

Today is the day for you to take the steps that you've been afraid to do.

Find your courage, put one foot in front of the other declaring that you're through.

Last, but not least, by all means never, ever consider harming yourself or suicide.

Every negative deed and word said about you, your abuser lied.

There are domestic violence hotlines, safe-houses and shelters that will help you to safely flee.

Once you've started over, not ever getting entangled in that life-style again is the key.

To Be Continued...

CHICKYPOOH™

About the Author

Jacqueline Charmane is an extremely talented, gifted, and anointed woman. In 1995, Jacqueline began performing nationally and internationally for theatrical productions. For nearly twenty-five years, Jacqueline has written, directed, and performed in stage plays, as well as designed spectacular fashions, costumes, and dance wardrobes. In 1998, Jacqueline began performing gospel comedy that after a decade gave rise to the character "Mother Maeye." Jacqueline (as Mother Maeye) has been seen on *Black Entertainment Television's* (BET) website, over a dozen commercials for the famous gospel talent show *"Sunday Best"*, and has two live DVD recordings. As an author and playwright, Jacqueline has written and published 13 books, 3 plays.

SPECIAL ACKNOWLEDGEMENTS
Illustration Characters' Contributors:
kakigori@123rf.com
3dmask@123rf.com
iimages@123rf.com
elvetica@123rf.com
blueringmedia@123rf.com
Yael Weiss@123rf.com
Shinya Fukazawa@123rf.com
blueringmedia@123rf.com
Summersun@123rf.com
Oleksii Ovchynnikov@123rf,com
Lorelyn Medina@123rf.com
dedmezay@123rf.com
Other Elements Contributors:
Clipart-library.com
Pnglibrary.com
Openclipart.org
Pngtree.com
Stickpng.com
Friendlystock.com

CHICKYPOOH™

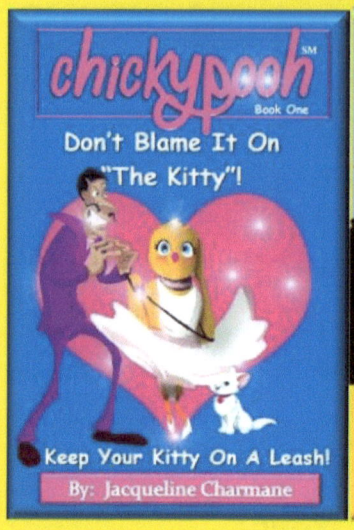